Monarch Butterfly of Aster Way

SMITHSONIAN'S BACKYARD

4

Bright August sunshine fills the
backyard of the white house
halfway down Aster Way. All is quiet
except for the *scritch-scratch* of a fox
squirrel and the buzz of some honeybees.
Under the rail of a shady gazebo, a new butterfly
clings to her chrysalis case. She slowly unfurls her
crumpled, scaled wings. They fan out around her,
orange and black, and quiver as she gathers strength.
She takes a few steps on her stiff little legs.

5

Then *whissssh*. As light as a whisper, Monarch lifts off, leaving behind the chrysalis that sheltered her during her change from fat caterpillar to slim butterfly. She drifts over the milkweed plants she had munched on, back in her caterpillar days. She flutters to coneflowers and zinnias and sips sweet, juicy nectar from each.

Monarch floats past the white house, over the white fence, and down Aster Way. She is beginning a long, danger-filled journey. She will fly south and west to spend her winter in Mexico, hundreds of miles away.

The sunlight begins to fade. Monarch lands on
a willow tree and hooks her tiny claws into the bark.
Without the warmth of the sun, her body becomes too
stiff for flight. She huddles close to four other butterflies.
They all fold their wings to wait out the night.

Late the next morning, Monarch basks on a sunlit rock. Warmed, she flits to some sunflowers, then visits some goldenrod. She sees their bright yellow colors with her bulgy, compound eyes and detects their scent with her knobby antennae. She tastes the flowers with her sensitive feet before she uncoils her proboscis and sips nectar—as if drinking through a small straw. She gets water from puddles in the same way.

11

Monarch flutters and soars, growing stronger each day.
She flies fast and far. Sometimes, wings outspread, she spirals
up, up, up on currents of air. Then, like a glider, she sails south
on high, speeding winds.

At times, other monarch butterflies join her. Together,
they skim over hills and lakes, towns and cities, forests and
fields. At night and on gray, rainy days, Monarch roosts.

One cool, drizzly day, Monarch clings to a fencepost, her folded wings hiding her colors. From high in a tree, a hungry blue jay spots her and dives toward her dark shape. Monarch struggles to fly, but she's too chilly and stiff. She drops to the ground. When the jay sees her spread wings, it swerves and swoops off, as if warned by Monarch's bold orange-and-black: *This butterfly is not good to eat!*

Monarch creeps back to the fence and hides under a rail to wait until the weather turns sunny once more. The next day is fine and she takes to the air.

15

One balmy September afternoon, Monarch reaches Washington, D.C. She floats over a green park, past a red stone castle, toward flowers growing beside a long walkway. She has come upon the Smithsonian Institution's butterfly garden.

Butterflies of many kinds flutter and fan their wings. Monarch drifts down and lands on a soft yellow patch. But it's not a flower—it's a sunhat! The child under the hat sits very still. Monarch rests there for a moment, then flits to some purple joe-pye weed. She stays and feeds a long time in the butterfly garden before she sets off again, south and west.

Butterfly
Habitat
Garden

On a breezy day in October, Monarch feeds beside a wide Texas highway with hundreds of other monarch butterflies. Cars and trucks whiz and whip by. Suddenly, a gust from a van sweeps her into the road. Monarch flaps hard in the swirling air. A huge truck zooms close and a strong blast of air tosses her high, then tumbles her into the grass at the road's edge. Monarch picks herself up, lifts off, and soon leaves the busy highway behind.

TEXAS

Monarch flies on, day after day. Finally, in mid-November, she reaches mountains in south central Mexico. She finds her way to a forest of oyamel trees. There, she joins millions of other monarchs to overwinter until spring. They cluster so closely, the trees look as if they might be sprouting butterflies!

Monarch finds herself a spot on a tree trunk and clings tight to the bark. She rests all winter long, using slight energy. She stirs now and then to bask or to feed—but only when the winter sun warms her enough to flit from her roosting place.

Snow falls. Storms come and go. A few branches break. But hardy Monarch survives.

At last, warm spring sunshine comes to the mountain. Then clouds of butterflies lift like smoke puffs from the oyamel trees. Monarch, too, stirs, flies, and seeks nectar in early wildflowers. As her strength is renewed, she flutters and swoops with the others. Sometimes she and a partner swirl high in the sky in a spiraling mating dance.

Soon, the butterflies sense that it is time to head north.
Monarch's body is heavy with eggs. She stops often to rest
and to feed. Whenever she finds a milkweed plant,
she lays her creamy eggs on its leaves,
one tiny egg at a time.

When Monarch reaches north Texas, her long journey is over. She is eight months old—very old for a butterfly—and it's time for her life to end.

But it's also time for new life to begin. Monarch's eggs will hatch, a few at a time, about a week from the day they are laid. The little caterpillars will eat milkweed for a month, maybe longer. When they become big and fat, they will form chrysalis cases around themselves. Sheltered inside, they will change into new monarch butterflies.

The new monarchs will fly north, sipping nectar from flowers, mating, and laying their eggs on milkweed plants. All along the way, eggs will hatch into caterpillars that become butterflies that keep traveling north, leaving *their* eggs behind.

More new butterflies will fly on until, by late August, one of Monarch's great-great-great-grandchildren might begin life in the sunny backyard on Aster Way—just as Monarch did.

About the Monarch Butterfly

Monarch butterflies are known for their bold tiger coloring. The orange-and-black pattern warns birds and other predators that these butterflies are not good to eat. There are poisons from the milkweed plant in all monarch butterflies' bodies and wings.

Monarchs are the only butterflies that migrate to one special place and then start back in the spring. Nobody yet knows how monarchs find their way south to Mexico's Sierra Madre mountains. It could be by smell or by the sight of landmarks on the ground. They may use the sun as a compass, or somehow feel the pull of the earth's magnetic fields.

Scientists *do* know that without the oyamel forests in the Sierra Madre mountains, monarchs could not survive the winter. The climate there is just right. It is cool enough to slow down their body functions and warm enough so they do not freeze.

The Mexican government protects parts of the oyamel forest by not allowing trees to be cut down and by making sure the butterflies are not disturbed during their November-to-March resting time. If you want to help monarchs and attract them to your yard, plant a patch of milkweed in a warm spot.

Glossary

chrysalis: The stage of development in which a caterpillar changes into a butterfly. The monarch's chrysalis has a hard outside shell with golden spots.

compound eyes: Bulging eyes made up of thousands of tiny, six-sided lenses that let butterflies and other insects see a wide range of colors and movements.

overwinter: To survive the harsh weather of the winter months.

oyamel tree: A fir tree that grows in the highest forests of Mexico's Sierra Madre mountains.

proboscis: A thin, hollow tube on the front of a butterfly's head. It can reach far into a flower to sip nectar and roll up when not in use.

roost: To perch for the night or to settle down for rest or sleep.

Points of Interest in this Book

pp. 10-11: American toad.

pp. 14-15: gladiator grasshopper; helianthus.

pp. 24-25: older monarch butterfly, as indicated by his ragged-edged wings.

pp. 26-27: eastern milkweed bug (left); monarch butterfly egg under milkweed leaf; japanese beetle (right).

pp. 28-29: monarch caterpillar preparing to transform into a chrysalis.

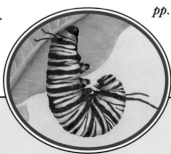